The
FOXMAN

The
FOXMAN

by Gary Paulsen

VIKING

VIKING
Published by the Penguin Group
Viking Penguin, a division of Penguin Books USA Inc.,
375 Hudson Street, New York, New York 10014, U.S.A.
Penguin Books Ltd, 27 Wrights Lane, London W8 5TZ, England
Penguin Books Australia Ltd, Ringwood, Victoria, Australia
Penguin Books Canada Ltd, 2801 John Street, Markham, Ontario, Canada L3R 1B4
Penguin Books (N.Z.) Ltd, 182–190 Wairau Road, Auckland 10, New Zealand

Penguin Books Ltd, Registered Offices: Harmondsworth, Middlesex, England

First published in the United States of America by Thomas Nelson Inc., Publishers, 1977
Published in simultaneous hardcover and paperback editions
by Viking Penguin, a division of Penguin Books USA Inc., 1990
1   3   5   7   9   10   8   6   4   2
Copyright © Gary Paulsen, 1977
All rights reserved

No character in this book is intended to represent any actual person;
all the incidents of the story are entirely fictional in nature.

Library of Congress catalog number: 90-50061
ISBN 0-670-83360-6

Printed in the United States of America
Set in Melior

The
FOXMAN

ONE

That first summer I was fifteen . . . the summer when the judge sent me to my Uncle Harold's farm up in northern Minnesota on the edge of the woods that went north forever.

I'd been there before, of course, but only to visit for a week now and then. We were pretty much town people, though I'd worked on farms in the summers, and they were farmers and woodcutters, and so after a little while there wasn't a whole lot to talk about. Or there wasn't then, but that was before I knew how they talked.

Then my folks decided to stay drunk all the time, in the summer when I turned fifteen. Well, actually I don't think they *decided* to do it because once when my father was being sick in the morning I heard him ask God not to let him drink anymore. But either God wasn't listening because he was puking, or it wasn't the sort of thing He did, because by three o'clock that afternoon my old man was drunk again and so was my mother—they started on beer and worked into bourbon—and that night my mother got me under the kitchen table and tried to kill me with a butcher knife.

Of course I knew it was only the booze, but I had to hop some to keep out of range and I got a few nicks in my arm when I tried to push the knife away.

The next thing I knew there were cops all over the place. The neighbors in the next apartment had called them. And the morning after that, the judge looked at my arm, said some things about my folks that were pretty strong, and sent me up to my Uncle Harold's place.

"You will stay there until the court decides on the fitness of your home," he said. Then he gave Harold—who'd come down to pick me up—one of those heavy looks, the kind that is supposed to mean a lot, and we walked out of the courtroom.

It was only sixty-five miles from the courthouse to Harold's farm, but it seemed to take forever in the old '38 Ford pickup with the springs poking up through the seats. The muffler was shot, or maybe it was the manifold, and even cruising down the highway the noise was so loud you could hardly hear yourself think.

I stared out at the country as we drove—thick woods and cleared fields here and there—and felt sorry for myself. I'd been sent away from home before, twice for short times because of the booze, and it was never nice. Never. Even going to Harold's farm, which was a nice place, with his two kids—my cousins—Carl and Don, and Aunt Mildred, who could cook like anything, and old Hans and Agile, Harold's father and uncle, who sat around all winter telling stories about the way things used to be—even with all that it would have been better to stay at home.

But of course I couldn't say that to Harold, not really; not with him being good enough to take me in and all.

Only Harold was pretty sharp, pretty savvy, like they say up north, and I think he knew how I was feeling because when we'd gone about halfway, clanking and sputtering down the road, he leaned over.

"Got a room all cleaned for you." He had to yell over the engine. "Upstairs on the south side of the house—the windows give good sun."

I nodded but didn't look at him.

"Be warm."

I let that one hang.

"Be nice in the winter."

I nodded again.

"Be your own room—ain't nobody going to bother you there."

"Thanks." I looked at him finally and tried to smile. "That will be nice."

We went back to silence then and I thought how it would be, only I didn't really know, but just

3

thought, the way you do sometimes. Dumb dreams—like how I'd get a lock for the door and not let anybody in unless I felt like it. Really stupid.

Pretty soon the trees closed in on the road and there were no more fields, just thick woods with bright-green low brush so tight you couldn't walk in it, all of it coming right to the edge of the highway. It was getting hard to look out the window with nothing to see but a green blur, so I faced the front.

"Woods," Harold said, pointing out the window with his chin. "Be from here to the farm now— just woods."

I nodded, remembering from the times I'd visited. The woods that went forever, they called it, and once on a big map I'd looked at it and between the lakes and forest it was huge, a wild place four hundred miles wide and going all the way up into Canada to the tundra line—over a thousand miles long. All woods.

"I got almost two hundred acres bucked clear now," Harold said. "Two hundred acres of black rich—be good dirt. Another three hundred acres are still in woods."

The truth was I didn't much care about farming, or how they had to clear the land up in the north to be able to farm. None of it made much difference right then, but I smiled and said having two

4

hundred acres cleared was a pretty good chunk.

"Be all a man needs," Harold said, snorting a laugh. "But then if I keep having pups I'll probably need more."

Right about then the road widened and we came onto a small store, bar, and gas station, kind of hunkered in the trees.

"Holt's place," Harold said, pulling over. "Be the last store on the way and I need snoose."

We got out and went into the store, which was more than a store and had traps and guns and dusty furs and stuffed moose heads mixed in with the grocery and hardware junk.

An old woman came from the rear somewhere—I found out later her name was Widow Holt—and waited on us without talking. She never said a word, not even when Harold paid for the snoose—and a sackful of candy for Agile and Hans—and when we got into the truck I asked how come she didn't talk.

"Hasn't said a word since her old man got killed—be ten, no, fifteen years now, I guess. Damn, it seems like yesterday."

"How'd he die?"

"Moose. Old cow moose with a calf—stomped him into jelly. I helped put him back together for the burying." He snorted and put snoose from the new can in his lower lip, spit out the window. "Never seen the like—be like a train ran over him."

I tried to picture it, dying with a moose jumping on you, and it didn't come out right. I'd had a Holstein bull come at me once, but he was big and mean looking. Moose were all angles and seemed to be too dumb to be able to hurt you.

"How'd it happen?"

Harold shifted before answering, his big red hand coming off the wheel to work the shift as he backed up. "Old man Holt was cutting wood pulp, for the paper mills down south. He dropped a tree right across where the old cow had her calf hid and it killed the calf." He shrugged. "Only the calf whimpered when it died and she heard it and came a-running. Be five of us in the woods with Holt, not too far away, either, but before we could get to him that old lady had stomped him down and killed him."

"Bad way to die."

Harold slowed the truck and turned off on two ruts that went away into the trees. It was getting late in the afternoon and in between the trees it was almost dark. "Be four more miles to the farm, all rough—you got to wet a stump?"

I shook my head. "No, I'm all right."

Which was only partly true. I mean I didn't have to go to the bathroom, but I wasn't all right, either. Moving to a new home because the court made me when my old home, no matter how bad it was, was a *home*—it wasn't all right at all.

But that was before I knew that I would be living at Uncle Harold's for over two years, before I knew I would become part of the family and get to like it better than my old home, before I learned to live in the woods until *that* was like a home, too.

And it was before I met the Foxman. Which wasn't really his name, only I never heard any other name. But that doesn't matter because people like the Foxman never need real names—what they are is more important than what you call them, somehow.

TWO

Looking back, now that I'm seventeen and able to understand some things, I can see that they really tried to make me fit in at Harold's place.

When we pulled into the yard it was dark, soft summer dark, but the whole family came out to the truck anyway. Even Agile and Hans, who were old and normally wouldn't care too much about just another kid. Mildred hugged me and said how glad she was to see me, which might not have been true because the last time I was there I conned Carl—who was then only eleven or so—into peeing on an electric fence and Mildred half beat me to death with a two-by-four. But it was a nice start, and even Carl didn't bear a grudge and came up to me and wrestled me a little. Don hung back because he was still young and shy, but he smiled before looking away.

Agile and Hans studied me in the dark for a couple of minutes, then Hans turned away, but Agile said, "Going to have to put meat on him to get any work out of him."

I was running a bit thin at that, what with not eating too regularly, but I was all right for work and told him so.

He "hummphhed" and went into the house.

"Come on." Carl picked up the box I had with all my clothes and junk in it. "I'll show you your room."

They'd done a job on the room. It was upstairs on the south side, like Harold had said, and it was clean and fresh painted in a kind of soft yellow that made everything feel warm and sunny even at night. There was a bed in the corner under the windows—covered with a thick quilt that was all patches—and a giant picture of a Hereford bull in a board frame just over the bed.

"The picture was my idea," Carl said, when he saw me looking at it. "I made the frame and everything."

"It's a good picture."

"Naaaww—it's a piece of junk. But it's the ony big picture I could find with a lot of color in it. I figured you'd need a colorful picture to look at—cheer you up. I mean . . ."

"I know what you mean." He was getting embarrassed. "It's all right."

"Was it pretty rough?"

I shrugged. "They just can't quit drinking."

Carl ran his hands through his hair. It was thick

and curly blond and kept falling in his eyes.
"That's hard to understand."

He meant it, too. Like he couldn't understand
how they could get hooked on it and not be able
to break it. I couldn't either.

"I heard she stuck you with a knife." He tried
to keep his voice regular, but I could tell he was
dying of curiosity. "Did it hurt?"

"No—she just went crazy, is all. Kind of cut my
arm. A little."

He waited for me to say more and when I didn't
he turned away. "Come on—supper's almost ready
and Mom will skin us if we're late."

I followed him back down the stairs and that
was the last time anybody in that house asked a
single thing about my folks, which was nice. I
think maybe Harold got a note now and then from
the court, or whoever it was that kept an eye on
things, but I never saw anything, so I couldn't be
sure.

When they ate at Harold Peterson's, they ate.
When we went into the kitchen, Mildred had the
big table with the benches all set up. Hans was at
one end and Agile at the other, because they were
older and got the end chairs, and the rest of us sat
on the benches on the side.

The table was covered with platters full of food,
so if you didn't know them and walked in during

the meal you'd think they were rich. But it was all food they made themselves. Like there was a huge plate of corn, and another one of meat piled high, and a crockery bowl so big a kid could take a bath in it was full of whipped potatoes. And then there were peas and string beans and cucumbers in vinegar and rich gravy and fresh rolls and choke-cherry jelly.

And none of it came from a store. None of it. The vegetables all came from the garden, and the potatoes they grew, and the corn was sour field corn raised for feed for the cattle—only picked early so it was still sweet, and the jelly was from berries picked by Carl and Don.

The meat was from a moose, and it tasted every bit as good as prime beef—you couldn't tell the difference. "Woods-meat," they called it, and they never ate anything else, never killed their own stock.

The meal was silent except for the sounds of eating—chewing and clinking of silverware. Nobody talked until the meal was over and the table was empty. Then Hans—who had homesteaded the farm and who was still the head of the family—leaned back and rolled a cigarette out of Velvet pipe tobacco and sighed.

"Thank you, God," he said, "for a bountiful meal, and thank you, Mildred, for cooking it."

That was it, graced and done, and as the weeks and months went by it never changed. Only what happened after the meal changed. In the summer when everybody was done eating the grown-ups went into the living room and talked about work for an hour—talked about the farm. Which was pretty boring and would put you to sleep faster than a pill.

In the winter the grown-ups went into the living room and sat by the stove telling stories. And that wasn't boring, but could keep you awake half the night—especially later when the stories started getting to me so I had to think about them.

But I didn't know that the first summer, that first night, and after dinner when the grown-ups went into the living room Carl grabbed my arm and took me upstairs back to my room.

Mostly we just sat around and talked about junk that night, and listened to the moths slapping against the window.

Carl told me all about Sharon Emerson, who lived on a farm two miles away and who was sixteen but looked older and was pretty developed. Carl told me he kissed her once earlier in the spring and she'd kissed him back, so I told him about a girl I'd known in town who'd kissed back.

That kind of junk. And we giggled some, laughed at nothing the way you do, until Mildred came upstairs and told us to stop or she'd nail both of us, and about ten minutes after that Don came in and we started to wrestle.

But quiet-like, and only on the bed, so we wouldn't thump around on the floor and bring Mildred back up again. When we got tired of that we just lay back and turned off the lights and listened to the night birds singing while I asked about the farm and what we would have to do.

"Tomorrow we buck while Dad gets the crops in," Carl answered.

"Buck? What's that?"

"Clear land," Carl said. "The three of us take the team out and clear land."

I thought about it for a minute or so, wondering. "Bucking—is it hard work?"

Carl laughed in the darkness. "Tomorrow night you're going to be so tired that if Sharon Emerson kissed you, you couldn't kiss her back."

"Too pooped to pucker," Don said, which was all right even if he was just a kid, and we started laughing again. That brought Mildred up because it was almost ten, and it happened two more times before I finally went to sleep and dreamed about my folks.

THREE

We bucked all summer.

And it was hard work, harder even than Carl had said, so hard that in two weeks I was tougher than I'd ever been, and had enough meat on me even to make Agile happy.

There was this ten-acre patch on the north side of the farm, and that's where we worked. All summer and into the fall, the three of us—though Don was too young to be much help—bucked and grubbed and hacked until those ten acres were ready for the plow. Which maybe doesn't sound like an awful lot, when you consider that a bulldozer can do ten acres in four days. But we didn't have a bulldozer, and even if there'd been one around, Harold couldn't have afforded it because he didn't do things with money the way they do in town.

We had a team of workhorses—Jim and Digger, two of the biggest geldings I'd ever seen—and we jerked every stump in that ten acres. It was rough, but not bad either because the grown-ups were at the other end of the farm, working on crops with tractors and didn't bother us except to ask at supper how much we'd done.

We'd get up in the morning and tie into a breakfast that was bigger than some people's Sunday dinners, then out to the barn by six to harness the team. At first I didn't know what I was doing, and slapping all that leather and chain on those two walls of horse seemed impossible. But then Carl showed me how it was all easy. You just start with buckling the collar on, then the hames, and work on back to the tail strap. Jim and Digger were what Carl called "baby-nice," and didn't mind us jacking them around at all but kind of leaned over on one leg in back, the way big horses do, and let us take our time.

Pretty soon I could harness and drive them as good as Carl, and not long after that Jim and Digger kind of took over so we didn't have to do anything but point them at a stump. They were sharp, and could pull like ten tractors. I've never seen anything like it, not before and not since.

The ten we were clearing had been logged off for pulp a few years before, so all the big trees were cut down, but the stumps were still there and that's what bucking is—working those stumps out of the ground.

And they don't want to come—not ever. Sometimes the roots go down and spread out ten or fifteen feet, as mean and tough as snakes, and the only way to buck the stump is to dig down and cut the roots with an ax. Then you back the team in and throw a chain from the doubletree back around the stump, a chain with links as big as your arm, and slap Digger and Jim on the rump.

"Ho, Jim, *pull!*" we'd holler. ""*Up*, Digger, you lame-brained good-for-nothing—heave your guts out!" And more like that, hard words but soft sounds because that's what they were used to— what Hans called music.

And their back legs would ripple with power, just wild shots of muscle that went up and down like meaty lightning. Then they'd get into it *hard* and you could see their hooves sinking into the ground with pull while they held their breath and heaved until you thought they'd bust their hearts or die right there in the traces hanging on the stump.

And up she'd come. Roots snapping and breaking so loud it was like gunfire, the stump would loose and come out all covered with fresh black dirt and angleworms and rotted wood, filling the air with a rich new smell that I could never understand, a kind of black-earth smell.

Then the team had to be blown, which meant

you had to let them stand and breathe easy for a few minutes to get over the strain of pulling.

Funny—now, looking back, we never talked while the team was blowing, just stood. Even Don, who talked a lot, stared at the stump and where it came from in silence. It made us feel solemn or something, like we'd done something almost wrong, jerking the old stump out of the ground. On a good day we might take four or five stumps, big ones, jerked out of the ground, and in all those jerks while we bucked all summer we stood silent when the horses were blowing.

Never said a word.

Of course we did a lot of other stuff that summer. They never worked on Sundays at Harold's—they didn't go to church or Bible read, but they never worked, either—and so Sundays we'd go do things we thought were fun.

There was this pool down below the barn on the south side of the pasture that was more mud than water, and we'd go down and swim naked in it when the afternoons were hot. It was all right except that the mosquitoes hung back in the brush while you stripped and then nailed you for fair between clothes and water. If you weren't fast you'd be all over welts and be up half the night scratching.

Sometimes we'd ditch Don, and Carl and I

would go riding on Jim and Digger—which wasn't like riding horses but more like sitting on big tables that could move—off down the country roads. That sounds good, and looks good in those pictures you see on calendars all the time where the kids are riding the horse under big trees.

But the truth is that blackflies follow the horses, and so do deerflies. Clouds of them. And they bite like the very devil, hurting and itching at the same time, and by the time you've gone a mile down one of those pretty country roads all covered with trees you're wondering if you're going to get home alive. And then you've got to rub all over with baking-soda paste to stop the itching.

I think we went riding like that two or three times—which shows how dumb we are—and every time it turned into a race between us and the flies. And we always lost.

Toward the end of summer the flies went back to wherever they came from—and not a moment too soon, for my money—and after that it got so you could stand it in the woods.

That was about when Carl took me over and introduced me to Sharon, whom he hadn't lied about at all and who was pretty developed and who did more than kiss me back. Which was all right, but I don't want to go into it because if it ever got back to Mildred she'd have my guts for a clothesline. Mildred is a nice aunt, but narrow in some ways, especially when it comes to boys and girls in clover fields, and there's no sense in talking about something that will get me in trouble. Especially after I gave Don a perfectly good belt and ten whole dollars to keep his mouth shut about Sharon and some other things that wouldn't sit too well with Mildred.

Carl got by without giving Don money because he told him he'd smother him in the manure pile in back of the barn if he said a word about it. But they're brothers and Carl could get away with a threat where I couldn't.

And that was pretty much how we spent the summer—working and staying out of trouble, just. Then it got to be September, and school, which wasn't anything but a room with a bunch of kids in it—not at all like school back in the city—and not long after that the leaves turned, splashed color around so wild it almost hurt your eyes to see it, reds and yellows that just burned in the sun.

It was fall, and two weeks into fall it froze.

"It come a frost last night," is how Hans said it to Harold the next morning at breakfast. "It come a hard frost, first of the year."

Harold looked up from his eggs. "Yah. Be fall now, be winter soon."

Hans sipped some coffee and smacked it around in his mouth. He drank it sweet, with four spoons of sugar in it—almost thick. "Always one week after the first hard frost it's time to kill."

Harold nodded. "I figure to go out next Sunday."

Hans smiled and I saw Carl across the table flash the same smile.

"Good," Hans said, rolling his cigarette. "I've been craving fresh liver."

FOUR

I used to go hunting back when I was living in town with my folks. I had an old .22 single-shot and every weekend I'd hit the woods. But that was different from how Harold hunted. I just went out and plunked around, trying for rabbits or maybe grouse if they didn't fly and I could get a shot. I sort of used it to get away for a day now and then. Like fishing.

Harold went for meat. There was no sport to it— which is kind of dumb, anyway. Calling hunting a sport, like they do back in town where they go out once a year with a high-powered rifle and blow the guts out of a defenseless deer.

Harold took Carl and me out that Sunday morning, clanking through the frost in the '38 Ford truck down the roads.

"Be a stand of alfalfa down a mile," he said, spitting snoose. "They come out to feed."

I was some excited, but Carl seemed calm and even bored. He was holding the rifle, an old lever-action .30-.30 that had probably been in the family since Hans was young. It had been cleaned so many times that all the blueing was worn off the barrel. When we'd gone about a mile Harold stopped the truck and got out, using a finger to keep us quiet. He carefully stuck two shells in the rifle, worked one into the chamber and let the hammer down easily to safety cock.

Then he walked down the road ahead of us. By this time I was shaking like a leaf. I'd never killed anything bigger than a rabbit and had a first-class case of buck fever. I didn't know it then, but Hans told me later that night.

Suddenly Harold stopped, raised the rifle and fired twice off to the right of the road. I never saw a thing. Just "crack-crack" and he waved us out ahead of him into a small field of alfalfa off to the right and front. And there were two dead deer, not just down but *dead*, with their heads half taken off.

I mean it was some shooting. They didn't even twitch, just *bam* and down and dead.

Harold handed Carl the rifle and pulled a hunting knife out of his back pocket and cut them open and I turned away.

I wasn't sick, really, it's just that I wasn't ready for all the blood. It seemed like gallons of it, more than you'd expect from something as small as a deer; all red and thick and rich in the still green alfalfa.

It just took a second or so and I had it under control, but Carl saw me and smiled. "You still got a city nose."

But it was all right, it wasn't teasing, just saying something because it was true, so I nodded and smiled, and it was over.

When Harold had dropped the guts he took both hearts and the livers and wrapped them in fresh grass. Then we loaded the two carcasses and the hearts and livers into the back of the truck and went back to the farm.

When we got there we helped Harold hang the dead deer in the cool room of the barn and spent the next four hours skinning them out, stretching the hides on the granary wall because later they could be sold when they were dry—for a dollar each—and two dollars was money.

And that was it.

"Be good to let them hang for two weeks," Harold said. "To age the meat and make it tender."

He wiped his hunting knife on the fatty part of one of the carcasses, to keep it from rusting, and carried the hearts and livers into the house for Mildred to cook up for Agile and Hans because old men need fresh blood-meat—at least that's what Harold said. But I noticed that he tucked away a good chunk of liver that night, when Mildred fried it up with fresh-cut onions and slapped fried potatoes in a side dish, so it probably wasn't just for the old men. I tried it and it tasted all right, but I kept thinking of the blood when Harold had cut the deer open—just couldn't get it out of my mind—so I didn't enjoy the liver the way I should have; and I couldn't eat the broiled heart at all.

After supper Carl and I went upstairs, because it was late and still too early in the year for the old men to tell stories—that didn't come until hard snow.

By this time Carl had moved into my room and left Don alone in what used to be their room, so we often talked until late before we fell asleep.

I flopped on the end of the bed. "That business today, hunting . . ."

"That wasn't hunting," Carl cut in. "That was killing."

"What's the difference?" I looked at him, hair hanging in his eyes. "We went out to get deer, and we got deer—or Harold did. That's hunting, right?"

He shook his head. "No—like I said, that's killing. Dad just went out for meat and took it—there's no hunt to it. Generally grown-ups don't hunt, 'specially when they've been to war, like all the men here."

"All of them?"

Carl threw me a quick nod. "Hans and Agile fought in the First World War, Dad in the Second.

26

You'll hear all about it this winter when they start the stories." He shook his head. "*Man*, will you hear about it—every night."

"Oh—well, fine." But I was still hung up on the other thing. "What's the difference between killing and hunting?"

He laughed. "Come first good snow, first real winter storm, you'll know."

"What do you mean?"

"Because that's what we do all winter up here— hunt. Go to school, do chores, and hunt. I didn't go into it before because I didn't know how long you were going to be up here. Now that it looks like you might be staying awhile we'll get into it."

"What do you—I mean we—hunt?"

"Almost everything," he said. "Wolves, rabbits—to sell to the mink farms down south, for food. Bear, if they aren't sleeping winter down and we can get one. Fox—well, we can try for fox but they aren't so easy to get because they're smart." He shrugged. "Mostly rabbits. They're worth fifty cents apiece."

"I don't have a gun—how do we hunt?"

"No sweat, we'll pick you up a twenty-two." He thought for a minute. "Yeah, and we'll have to get you a parka and make you some skis."

"Make skis?"

"Sure. I've got some birch slats from over a year ago. They ought to be good and dried out by now—

it only takes a couple of days to make a good set of skis.''

I had my head back on the bed and happened to be looking out the window. "Well, the way it looks, we'd better get on that tomorrow after school."

"Why?"

"Because it's snowing. Hard."

We both got up and went to the window, looked out at the big flakes drifting down; they were wet and fell straight. Some of it would melt off, but a lot of it would stay until the next snow.

Winter had come.

"Funny," Carl said, "it's really funny."

"What—snow?"

"No. Yes, in a way. Every time we kill in the fall, it snows that night. Every time."

"Really?"

He nodded, watching the snow. "Every time."

So we watched it snow for a while without talking and it was the same kind of silence as we had when we'd just jerked a stump and the horses were blowing, the kind you don't really think about too much because it's hard to understand and thinking about it seems wrong, somehow.

FIVE

Working on those birch skis made me want to be a carpenter, even though I knew it was one of those things that would go away, like wanting to be a pro hockey player in the winter or a teacher because one of your teachers was all right.

Thing is, at Harold's place if you wanted something you *made* it—there was no running to the store. All the farms up there were that way; like if you needed a new table you went out in the granary and fired up the potbelly so it was warm and you made a table. You didn't call the store and have them deliver one.

And the same for the skis. Up north in the woods the snow—the stay-snow, like they call it, because it's there all winter—gets really deep. Sometimes it's over eight feet, and I've heard of twelve, and that's not drifted but just what fell. Without skis you just sink in, and keep sinking, and those store skis they make for cross-country are too small to do much good.

So you make your own skis.

Carl showed me what to do, because he'd made them before. Hans had taught him how it was done back in the old country, which would be Norway, but they always called it the old country.

We started with two birch boards about four inches wide and five feet long and maybe half an inch thick. They were dry and hard and uncracked, like Carl had said—he had them stored in the rafter ties in the granary. I used a coping saw and cut the tips, which were still flat, so they rounded in, with a snow-cutting tip on the end.

Then for the next day I used a rasp, sitting in the granary with the stove going while it stormed and dropped to almost zero outside, and I worked the wood down on the tops to lighten them but keep them strong with a kind of inverted belly that ran the length of the skis. I left a flat place for the bindings, just a leather cup that held the front of the foot, and then flopped them and used a special gouge that Hans gave us to make the steering grooves down the middle of the bottom.

"Not bad," Carl said, when I'd finished and sanded them so they were like glass on the bottoms. "Not great—but not bad. Now we've got to curl the tips."

"I've been wondering about that."

"It's the easiest part."

He got a barrel with about a foot of water in the bottom, an old oil drum with the top cut out, and set it on the potbelly. Then he put the skis in so the tips were in the water.

"You just boil them for about three hours, so the tips are good and soft, then slap them in a bending jig, and let them dry for two days."

So we sat out there in the granary and fired the stove hotter with cut birch, which burns like coal—only it doesn't stink—and boiled the skis.

Of course we talked, some about Sharon because she had to leave school. Everybody was talking about it and I was a little worried, but Carl said she was going to marry Richard Brennar, who was older and had a car and it had been too long for me to worry anyway.

Don sat there with big ears through all of it, so we had to talk around what we really meant, because sure as blazes if he knew he'd blab it to Mildred. He was just getting into the blabby stage then—right about eight years old. That's when kids start to talk a lot.

When the skis had boiled long enough, after I'd split and run about fifteen cords of birch through the stove to keep it hot, or it seemed like that much, Carl pulled them out and tried to bend them against the wall.

They gave and squished water out of the sides.

"Just right." He reached back up to the rafter ties and brought down a wooden curved mold.

"Hans made it years ago," he told me while he

put the ski tips in the mold and screwed the clamps down. "When he was cutting wood in the north woods."

I watched, waiting for the tips to break but they didn't; they just squeezed around the mold until it was tight and they were curved.

"Now we let them dry, and we can't look at them for two days."

"Why is that?"

He shrugged, sliding the skis with the mold on the end back up into the rafters. "I don't know. It's what Hans says—you can't look at them for two days, until they're dry. If you look, the tips won't set right and you'll have to do it over."

"That's silly."

He laughed. "Maybe—maybe not. It comes from the old country and you know how that goes. I just do it like he says and they'll come out right."

We turned the dampers down on the stove and closed the grates. I started out of the granary but Carl hung back.

"What's the matter?" I asked.

"Nothing. Just double-checking to make sure there isn't anything wrong—like hot coals out of the stove that might cause a fire. You know."

I waited and when it was all right we went into the house. It was dark, about five in the evening, and there was school the next day, so we had to eat and get to bed early. It was a mile walk out to where the bus picked us up and we had to be there waiting at six-thirty.

We ate and went upstairs. The winter stories hadn't started yet—Carl said they wouldn't until hard winter set in, which I didn't understand then but found out later—so there wasn't any reason to stay downstairs. I was shot, for no real reason, and hit the sack feeling tired but something was bothering me and finally I nudged Carl.

"You awake?"

"Yeah," he answered. "Sort of—what's up?"

"We're about the same age, right?"

"You woke me for that?"

"No. It just hit me, we're about the same age but you act a lot more grown-up—older."

"What do you mean?"

"Oh, like the bit with Sharon and all. You act more grown-up about it. Or the stove and the business in the granary about checking about fires."

"So?"

"Why is it that if we're the same age you act older?"

He didn't say anything for a minute. "I don't know—never thought about it."

"Well. You do."

"Yeah, I guess I do at that, but I don't mean to be that way. It just happened."

"Could it be something from living out here in the woods? On the farm?"

Again he was silent, then he sighed. "Yeah, maybe. There isn't much time to be a kid out here."

"What do you mean?"

"I don't know, really. It's just that back in town they kind of watch out for you and take care of you so you don't grow up so fast. Or something. Out here when you get old enough to work, you kind of have to grow up. It just happens."

"Because of the work?"

"Yeah." I could feel him nod in the darkness. "There's a lot to do. Grown-ups don't have time for a lot of child watching or whatever you call it."

"Will it happen to me? Because I'm living here?"

He waited before answering. "I think it already has—why, does it worry you?"

"No. I want it." I lay back and thought about it. "I want it very much."

"Better not think about it," Carl said, laughing.

"Why not?"

"Because it's probably like the ski tips. If you watch it or you think about it, it will come out wrong." He snorted. "That's what Hans would say, and Agile, and they're right an awful lot."

So we didn't talk anymore, but went to sleep. Or Carl did, because I could hear him breathing slow and easy in the dark next to me.

But I didn't sleep right away. I stayed awake and thought about growing up for a long time, thought how it would be to act like Carl or even older, which was all kind of dumb, I guess. But that's what I did, and when I finally got to sleep, there was a moon coming out across the snow, white and open, so the inside of the room was a pale white-yellow and not at all ugly, but soft, and like home.

SIX

I'm not sure when things changed, or how it happened. It seems like one minute I was still new at the farm, in the woods, and the next it was like I'd never been anywhere else.

It doesn't make sense, but about three weeks after I finished the skis, Carl and I were working the woods about five miles east of the farm on a Saturday morning in two feet of snow and we were setting traps for weasels and it was like I'd been doing it all my life.

That was about when I quit thinking of my folks all the time. I'd been dreaming about them almost every night—really stupid dreams, like how they'd quit drinking and were coming up to get me and take me home. Dumb dreams. But at the same time that I realized I wasn't new at the farm anymore, that I kind of fit in, I quit dreaming about them and only really thought about them when I was tired or just before I went to sleep. And then it wasn't bad. I was only just kind of wondering how they were doing.

Of course a lot of it was the woods. Like I said before, I'd gone hunting on weekends just to get away, the way all kids do—or want to. But that was nothing, absolutely nothing compared to what Carl and I did.

We *lived* in the woods. I mean we went to school, but every weekend and every night after school we hit for the brush. And nobody said a thing, either. Harold and Mildred just let us go, more or less, although we had to split birch every night for the stove before we left, and make sure the woodbox was full on the weekends before we cut out.

But as soon as the wood was cut we'd strap on our skis, using cut-off parts of truck inner tubes for clamps back around our ankles, hustle into our sweaters and our parkas and head on out.

The first couple of times we just took guns. I had an old twenty-two single-shot, the kind you had to pull back on before it would shoot, and Carl carried a break-open single-shot—an old sixteen-gauge shotgun that Hans gave him when he was eleven. But the guns were just for having. We didn't shoot anything those first few times, though I had a beauty of a crack at a fox that came out of a brush pile and hung in front of me for eight or nine seconds.

"Not prime!" Carl said, knocking the rifle up before I could shoot. "Let him go."

I got a touch mad at him. "There's bounty on him—four dollars."

He nodded. "Sure, but if we wait another month his coat will thicken out and we can get another two bucks for the hide."

And so it went, like they say up north. We'd go out and slide through the woods, sometimes only going a couple of miles, once making almost ten away from the house before we turned and came back.

Carl was figuring out where he should lay his trapline—which he ran for weasels and fox every winter because it made him some money—and I was learning. I was learning though I didn't know it, the way you can learn even though it doesn't seem you are, by having it rub off on you.

The first few times I was so dumb I didn't even know what questions to ask, and then it hit me that the best way to learn was to shut up and *not* ask, but just watch Carl.

Then one day, when we'd been doing it for three weeks, I laid a weasel set back under a broken root and I just *knew* it was right. Like I'd been doing it all my life.

I put the bait in back of the trap, stood up, brushed the snow off my pants and went on, busting through the snow with my skis like I owned the woods.

I mean I was *cocky*—too much, because when

you get cocky you miss a lot. But I didn't know that, then, and I caught up with Carl and we headed in because a storm was coming—you could see the black scout-clouds up north—and I was feeling some good, I can tell you, because maybe for the first time in my life I felt like I had a handle on something. I knew the woods, or thought I did, and it seems like knowing something makes you better. Maybe it doesn't, really, but it seems like it and that can get you through the day.

The storm hit that night, and it was a bomber. North wind ripped the tops of the trees, howling like some kind of wild thing, and the snow went by the house so thick you couldn't see the barn only a hundred feet away.

We ate supper—thin steaks from those deer, fried soft in butter—and the grown-ups moved into the living room. I started upstairs but Carl gave me a sign with his hand, so I hung back and we followed the grown-ups in by the stove.

It was time for the winter stories to start—the first real storm—and I could see that the living room had been changed around. The two soft chairs, the big ones, were set close to the stove with old coffee cans on the floor for spitting snoose, and the two short couches were drawn in close to the chairs.

Hans and Agile took the two big chairs and Harold and Mildred got on one couch, with Mildred on the end so she could go for coffee if she had to.

Carl, Don, and I took the other couch.

Then we just sat there, looking at the fire flickering through the little mica window on the front of the stove. I was full as a tick from the venison and potatoes, and feeling over-warm the way you get when you've been out all day and suddenly get too close to a stove, and in about thirty seconds I was having trouble keeping my eyes open.

"We was killing Chermans, then," Hans suddenly said—he meant Germans, but he said it "Chermans." "Over there in France."

I woke up and looked at him. He had his eyes closed, remembering how it had been. You could see the story in his face, somehow—lines moving as he thought.

"The mud was deep—up to your knees. And they shot big guns at us, cannon, until you couldn't hear or see, it was so bad." He paused to spit snoose into one of the coffee cans, and Agile nodded. He'd fought in France, too.

"So we was supposed to make an attack, and they blew the whistles and we came out of those trenches a-screaming and a-hollering and a-shooting." He laughed. "I don't s'pose we made two hundred feet and they shot those big guns and blew us all to hell."

Then he went on to say how he was blown into a hole full of mud and water and there was a guy on the other side of the hole. It was dark, so he couldn't really see the other man, but he talked to him and told him the whole story of his life because Hans figured for sure he was going to die and wanted somebody to know about his life.

In his story he talked to the man for what seemed like hours, and the man never answered, never made a sound, and finally he crawled over to the man and it was a dead German soldier.

"Yah!" he said, laughing and slapping his leg. "Dead as dead—he'd been dead for two, three days. Pretty lucky for me. I didn't get killed and some of the stuff I told him was pretty private. Pretty private. Being dead he couldn't tell anybody what I told him."

Well, then Agile laughed, and Harold and Mildred, and Carl, but I didn't because I was wondering how it could be that a dead man was funny, or the mud, or the cannons. None of it seemed funny to me.

But then I didn't know how it worked. It was a good story, fun to listen to because it was about war and war is always interesting, but I didn't think it was funny. Just kind of sad.

Later, of course, I found out that they didn't laugh because it was funny but because it was the kind of story you're *supposed* to laugh at; laughing was part of the story and without it the story wouldn't be right.

Sometimes that winter Hans told sad stories, too, so sad they made you want to cry and once in a while I'd look over and Mildred would be crying and even Don. And the crying was part of the story, just like the laughing was.

The thing I didn't understand was that all the stories were about war. All winter we listened to stories about the war—sometimes Hans and sometimes Agile would tell them—and I couldn't figure what it was that made them want to talk about war all the time. It was like war was a neat thing for them, a game they'd won or something—the only part of their life worth remembering or talking about.

I couldn't understand it then, even when I talked to Carl about it, and I understood it less later when I found out about the other part of war; the part nobody talks about.

The Foxman.

SEVEN

We had gone too far this time, too far north.

In the morning when we'd reached the outleg of the trapline we'd started to turn back, but a fox had jumped out ahead of Carl, who was breaking trail, and we'd gone after him because now they were prime and the money would be nice.

I tried a couple of shots with the rifle and missed, and we never got quite close enough for Carl to try the shotgun, which wouldn't be too good anyway because the pellets would hurt the hide and we'd get less when we took it into town to sell.

So we'd gone after him, plowing through the snow on his tracks, taking turns breaking trail because there was a foot of new snow on the two feet of old and it was murder if we didn't swap. As it was we could only make about a mile before dropping back and letting the other guy take over, and we must have done that eight or nine times at least.

And the fox stayed just ahead, always moving north. Soon we were in new woods even for Carl, following those dancing tracks, and when we came

45

THE FOXMAN

into a clearing Carl stopped so fast I almost ran
onto his skis.

"Gotta take a break," he said, blowing. "Figure
out how far we've come."

"He's getting tired, too," I said, pointing at the
fox tracks. "He's starting to stagger and his steps
are shorter." I wasn't so winded because I'd been
in back this mile. "I'll break for a while—we'll
have him soon." I started to move around Carl.

"No." He held up his hand. "We've come too
far. Look." He pointed in back of me, up to the
northeast.

I turned. There were clouds up there, black and
high—storm clouds. They looked mean. "So we
let the fox go?"

He nodded. "We'd better head back. Now. A
straight shot for the farm."

He was right, of course. We'd been following the
fox and he'd gone this way and that, always north
but back and forth across the line. "I figure if we
head just about away from that cloud we ought to
hit the farm."

"Me too." Again he nodded. "Only, how far is
it—can we beat the storm?"

"Not standing here, we can't." I pushed out
away from him, breaking trail southwest.

Funny, but when you're chasing something like
a fox you don't notice things—like how tired your
legs are, or how far a mile is when you're busting

46

a foot of snow. I'd gone about a mile when it hit me we'd never make it—no way. I stopped and turned to Carl.

He pulled up and nodded. We didn't need to talk—it was on both our minds. Coming on dark, a daddy of a storm coming in, and we were somewhere between fifteen and twenty miles from the farm in north woods.

"We'll have to make camp and ride it out," Carl said. "Going to be a long night."

"Yeah." I looked back at the cloud, which was a good four fingers above the horizon. "What about your folks—they get worried?"

He shook his head. "No—they know we can handle ourselves. We might get a whipping for being dumb enough to chase the fox, but they won't come after us."

"So." I let it ride, thinking. We had plenty of matches and there was dead and dry birch and poplar everywhere. "We'll need something to eat—a rabbit. And a good place to build a lean-to."

He nodded. "Let's keep working toward the farm until we find a good place—we can pick up a rabbit on the way."

We'd seen about a hundred snowshoe rabbits while we were chasing the fox, but we hadn't shot any because we didn't have time.

Now I broke trail more slowly, and in about a

hundred yards a snowshoe popped out in front of me and stopped the way they do, so I raised the rifle and squeezed a shot off.

The rabbit made a little leap in the air and fell and kicked for a few seconds, then died. I picked him up.

"We'll roast him later," Carl said. "It won't be too good without salt or anything, but it's food."

I nodded because I didn't feel like talking. It was always like that when I killed something—as if a lump came up in my throat or something. I didn't plan on it, or even feel bad, it just came and I wouldn't talk.

We skied for another mile or so, with Carl pulling the rabbit on a string behind him so it kind of jerked and skidded in the snow.

By now the cloud was overhead and there were snowflakes spitting around.

"If we're going to find a hole, we'd better do it soon."

Carl nodded. "Yeah. We'll have to get wood together for the night."

In front of us there was a swamp clearing, all snow over the deep grass, and on the other side there was a rise of ground without trees.

"Let's get up on that hump and look around. Maybe we can find an old tree down with an opening under it or something."

But when we got on top of the rise I looked down

and there was another small clearing, and on the other side of the clearing, against the trees, there was a small tar-paper shack. Next to it there was a huge woodpile, all cut and split, and in the flurries I could see bits of smoke coming out of the chimney on the shack.

I backed down on the rise and motioned to Carl to hold it. He'd been bringing up the rear.

"There's a shack down there, with somebody in it. What do you think?"

He skied past me and looked, then came back.

"I don't know. Might be a woodsy—some trapper up here. I saw some hides on the north wall of the shack. Fox hides." He shook his head. "I don't know who it could be—I've never been this far north, into the woods. As far as I know, nobody lives up here."

"But it's there."

"I see that."

"And it would be better than camping through this storm."

"Maybe."

"What do you mean—maybe?"

"Well, if it's a woodsy it would be all right, only . . ." He let it fall off.

"Only what?"

"Just stories. I've heard stories about men who live up in the woods because they can't be with other people. Men who have done things so they'd go to prison. If that's who lives in the shack, we could be in trouble."

We were suddenly hit with a gust of wind that lifted the edge of my parka. "Well, I don't care *who* it is, if they'll put us up for the night."

"Yeah, I guess you're right."

So we started down and skied across the clearing to the shack. As I got closer I could see yellow light coming through one of the double windows, from a kerosine lamp.

I felt kind of scared, but not really, and I was the first one to the shack, where I kicked out of my skis and leaned my rifle against the wall.

Then I reached up and knocked on the door.

I heard somebody moving inside, a kind of clumping around, then the door opened.

It was all I could do to keep from screaming and I turned away and looked down, half-sick, because the man who had opened the door was old, old like Hans, but besides that he was the ugliest thing I'd ever seen.

The face was scarred and twisted and kind of purple-paste looking and from the eyes down it wasn't really a face at all but like a nightmare with no nose and no lips so you could see the teeth like a skeleton.

I heard Carl gasp in back of me where he'd skied up, then the old man turned away and came back in a couple of seconds with a mask over the lower part of his face, a black cloth thing that covered everything but his eyes.

"Come in, come in," he said. "Out of this storm."

So we went into the shack because there really wasn't anything else to do.

EIGHT

The inside of the shack was dark except for the yellow light from the kerosine lamp. The lamp stood on a table that was covered with an oilcloth table covering with flowers on it.

I stared at the flowers to keep from looking at anything else and I noticed out of the corner of my eye that Carl was doing the same thing.

The room smelled, only not bad, but kind of rich and close—from cooking and smoking pipe tobacco—and in the gloom I could see books on shelves that filled one whole wall.

The old man had moved away, back in a corner by the bed, which was covered with a bearskin robe, so he was back in the dark.

"Sit—sit at the table," he said. "I'll make some coffee. And take off your coats and boots, or you'll get sick when you go back out."

I was all for leaving right then, and so was Carl, by the look of him, but the voice had been friendly and open—almost pleading—so I shucked out of my coat and boots, and when I started, Carl did the same.

Back in the dark corner of the shack he had a cookstove that also provided the heat for the room. He pulled a coffeepot onto the hot part of the stove and dumped some grounds in. Then he moved back to the bed.

I tried not to, but it was hard to keep from looking at him back in the gloom, hard not to look at the mask over the lower part of his face, even though it's wrong to stare and doesn't do any good anyway.

"So what are you doing in this neck of the woods during a storm?" His voice was only a little muffled by the mask. "Out for an afternoon stroll?"

There was a little laugh in his voice and Carl and I smiled.

"We were chasing a fox," I said. "And went too far north. But we aren't lost"—I added that kind of fast—"we aren't lost." It was dumb to get lost and I didn't want him thinking we were dumb, for no real reason except that I kind of liked his voice.

"No, I didn't figure you were lost," he said. "Just curious as to how you come to be out here."

"It was the fox," I repeated. "We shouldn't have followed him so long."

"They'll do that. Every time. Sharpest thing in the woods." The coffee boiled and he brought two cups over to the table and poured them full. Then he put a sugar bowl down with a spoon and went back to the bed.

Normally I'm not much on coffee, and neither is Carl, but we sipped it with plenty of sugar, to be polite, and it was all right.

"She'll be a mean storm," the old man said. "You spend the night before heading back. Where you from?"

So we told him our names and about the farm and all and he said he didn't know Harold, or Agile and Hans, but had come down from the north— up in Canada—and so wouldn't know too many people down south.

I wanted to ask him about a thousand questions, but they all seemed to have something to do with his face, or why he was living alone way out in the woods, and it didn't seem right to ask them.

So I just sipped my coffee and tried not to stare and instead looked down at the tablecloth. It was very old and worn, and the flowers on it looked blurred and hand-painted; in the glow from the lamp they looked almost real

"You read a lot." It was Carl—the silence was getting long and he never could handle long silences. "All the books on the wall?"

The old man nodded, his head moving up and down back in the dark corner. "Read all winter, in between checking my traps."

"You run a line?" I jumped on that. "What do you trap?"

"Foxes, mostly, some weasels."

"But what do you do with them?" I blurted it out. "I mean way out here . . ."

"Every spring I go out to the highway and meet someone who brings groceries and takes the furs. Once a year."

I whistled. I mean I couldn't help it. "Once a year . . ."

"I like living alone," he said, but he got it out too fast. "I've been out here ever since I got back from the war—or I should say out of the hospital. I like living alone out here in the wilderness—it gives me more time for my studies, for my books."

Again the conversation wound down, and I could hear the wind ripping outside the shack, tearing at the tar paper. He'd been right, it was cooking up to be a mean storm. It was lucky we'd found his shack, because holding it out under a tree would have been rough.

"Say, I'll bet you guys are hungry." He got off the bed and rattled some pans around the stove. "I've got some aged moose steak and fall potatoes that would sit right with you."

"No, that's all right." I tried to stop him. "We aren't hungry or anything."

But he wouldn't hear of it, even though I really wasn't hungry because I kept thinking of his face and how it had looked. It just stuck in my mind and I couldn't make it go away; it was so ugly. Like something off a monster you'd see in a movie, only worse because it was real.

So he cooked for a while, moving pans around and peeling potatoes back by the stove, while Carl and I looked at each other and away, the way you do, and I wondered what it was in war that could do that to a man's face and not kill him.

After a bit—it seemed like hours but was probably only thirty minutes or so—he put two plates on the table, heaped with steak and fried potatoes, and went back to his corner.

"Aren't you going to eat?" Carl asked.

"I ate before you came," he said, but I knew he was lying and guessed that he didn't want to eat when we were around because he thought it might make us sick.

Carl and I picked at the food and I managed to hold some down by thinking of other things, making my mind work on pleasant thoughts, and it was good food. The moose was aged and you could cut it with a fork, and he'd fried the potatoes in belly fat so they tasted like meat and stuck to your ribs.

When we'd finished he brought us more coffee and took the dishes away.

Then he went back to the bed and pulled out an old guitar and picked at it so that it made kind of pointless music, nice to listen to but it didn't go anywhere, only just rolled around.

"These are flamenco chords," he said. "From Spain. I like them after dinner."

And he went on playing until finally the food in my belly and the tiredness from the day mixed with the heat from the stove and the music, and I kind of leaned down on the table and went to sleep.

Carl must have done the same, because later in the night I opened my eyes and we were in the bed, covered with the bearskin, and the old man was sitting at the table reading by the light from the lamp, his face covered by the mask.

It didn't feel bad in the room, but close and friendly and warm under the bearskin, and I went back to sleep with a kind of fuzzy feeling—like it was weird that the old man and the shack were here when we needed a place to stay, weird but nice.

NINE

In the morning when we got up, he was already gone. There was coffee on the warm side of the stove, and some cold slices of moose meat on a plate on the table. Next to the plate was a note that said he had to go out on his line and was sorry to miss us but didn't want to wake us early because he thought we needed the sleep.

The note wasn't signed, and was written in proper English with periods and paragraphs. At the bottom it said: "cordially."

Cordially, I thought, cordially, the Foxman. Trapper of foxes.

"Let's get out of here," Carl said, finishing his coffee and heading for his boots. "This place gives me the creeps."

"Yeah, me too." I put my cup back and grabbed a piece of the moose meat, which I chewed while I worked into my boots. They were warm and dry from being by the stove all night and felt a little stiff.

It only took us a minute to get into our parkas

and get outside, where we brushed the night snow off our skis and got into the bindings.

The dead rabbit was still where we'd left it and Carl grabbed the string and started off first, breaking trail. I waited until he got out in front ten or fifteen feet and followed, letting my skis ride in his grooves.

We didn't say anything until we got to the top of the rise, heading southwest. Then Carl pulled up to catch his breath. It was deep cold, blue cold, they call it up north, like the inside of ice, and the first three or four hundred yards were almost painful—until our lungs got used to the chilled air.

"What do you think?" Carl squinted with one eye almost closed against the brightness of the new sun on the white snow.

"About what?"

He snorted. "About him, the old guy, that's what—what else would I be asking about?"

"I think it's sad. That's what I think."

He nodded. "Yeah. Sad."

"Let's go." I didn't understand it, but I didn't want to talk about the old man. "We've got a long ways to go."

Carl swung back and started off, but just before we topped the rise and started down I turned and looked back and I saw the old man come out from in back of the woodpile and go into the shack. He tried to make it without being seen, but I caught

his motion and turned away so he wouldn't know
I'd seen him.

He'd been hiding in back of the woodpile, waiting for us to leave. He'd made the coffee and
warmed the moose meat and gone outside and hidden behind the woodpile, even though it was probably fifteen or twenty below zero—just so we
wouldn't have to look at him.

Carl was up ahead and hadn't seen him. I started
to wave him down, or call to him, but then I
thought no, what good would that do? We couldn't
go back without embarrassing the old man, the
Foxman, and it wouldn't do any good to talk about
it with Carl. Not really.

So we skied. All day, moving through the morning and into the afternoon, plowing through new
snow and new cold, everything clean and white
and fresh.

And when I was in back I kept staring at the rabbit jerking on the end of the string tied to Carl. The
hole where my bullet had gone through was all purple and frozen against the white fur and I stared and
stared at the hole—jerk-stop, jerk-stop—because it
was something I didn't want to see and you always
stare at things you don't want to see.

The hole made me think of the Foxman's face,
and the war, and how it was that Hans and Agile
could remember the war the way they did, almost
happy, and tell all the stories they told when the

same war could do something like that to a man's face.

It was coming on dark when we finally skied onto the farm—dark and very cold. Maybe thirty-five below.

They had the Coleman lantern fired up in the kitchen and we could see the light when we were still a half a mile from the house and I stopped Carl.

"What's the matter?" His breath shot out white in the moonlight. "Why are you stopping this close to a warm room?"

"About the old man . . ."

"Yeah?"

"Let's not tell them about him. All right?"

"Why not?"

"Because he wants to stay private and all. If we tell the grown-ups about him, they'll probably go out there." I took a breath, felt it bite deep and cold. "It just wouldn't be right."

Carl thought about it for a minute. "Yeah, I guess you're right. We'll keep quiet about it."

He turned and we skied on into the yard and Mildred came out with Harold and she hugged us and Harold smiled—at first, because they were glad to see us. But then they decided we'd been wrong to stay out that way, and worry them, so Harold took us into the calf side of the barn and dusted us a little with his belt, only not hard, just enough so we'd know we'd been wrong.

He wasn't mean about it, just giving medicine, and when he got done he offered us snoose—knowing we didn't chew—because it was his way of making up.

"Be a long time waiting up for you," he said, hunkering down in the barn, filling his lip. "Worried the lady."

So we said we were sorry and told him how the storm caught us and we thought it would be best to ride it out, so we stopped. We didn't lie, quite, just didn't tell the whole story.

Then we went in and ate like a couple of kings because Mildred figured we were starving, which was pretty close to that, what with skiing all day without food.

And after we ate we went straight up to bed, because we were tired and because we had to, and I don't suppose we stayed awake thirty seconds before the tiredness caught up with us and we went under as if we'd been hit with hammers.

And all through it, until my eyes closed and I went under, through the dusting and the big supper and going upstairs to bed, I kept thinking of that rabbit jerk-stopping in front of me with the purple hole where my bullet had gone in when I killed him.

TEN

I'm not sure why I decided to go back and see the Foxman. It wasn't that I thought he wanted to see me—he'd been living out there too long alone to need company.

It might have been Carl. About two weeks after we spent the night in the shack Carl decided to fall in love and you know how that goes. Her name was Bonnie—Bonnie Anderson—and I guess she was all right, even pretty, but nothing to go hog wild over the way Carl did. He talked about her every night, all night, until I got so sick of listening I told him to shut up, which of course got him mad and we tussled around some but didn't really fight.

Then he started going over to Bonnie's a lot— not just on Saturday, or Friday night, but even on weeknights. Bonnie lived about three miles away, so Carl would take the old Ford truck and before I knew what was happening he was gone every night, coming back late and all glassy-eyed. Which might have been love, like he said, or it could be because the truck didn't have a heater and it was running thirty below some of those nights and he was freezing to death by inches.

I guess love is strong, like they say—I know *I* wouldn't have acted that lame-brained and giddy-up crazy over anything like Bonnie Anderson without being in love. Maybe not even if I was in love, looking back on it.

I swear, twice Carl came back with his ears so cold the white didn't go away when you pinched them—just short of mean frostbite and he would have lost the lobes except that we rubbed snow on them and thawed them slow, all without telling Mildred or Harold, or course. They would have put a stop to it fast if they'd known being in love was endangering Carl's health.

What with Carl being gone all the time I wound up running the line. Which was all right, because I got all the money for the weasel pelts and they were bringing almost a dollar each, plus the money from the rabbits I nailed while running the line.

I got over killing fast. It's one of those things you get used to, and pretty soon I was knocking over rabbits, even one fox, with the little .22 without a second thought. I was banging them down and cleaning the guts out right where I shot them and it didn't bother me a bit.

And I found that I liked working the line alone. Every night after chores I'd check the short leg, the little loop that ran down the creek in back of the barn for about a mile, and the first time I'll have to admit it was a little weird being alone in the woods at night. I wasn't scared, exactly, just a little more aware of sounds and movement.

But then I found I wasn't alone, that there were other hunters out—snow owls, and lynx, and night killers like weasels. Once I saw a wolf that was working a brush pile for rabbits, not a big timber wolf but the smaller brush kind, and he studied me for almost ten seconds before trotting off into the dark. He was all right, and I didn't shoot even though I had the rifle because wolves don't really bother much but sheep and Harold didn't have any sheep.

And like I said, I got to liking it in the woods alone when I found that there wasn't anything waiting to kill me. I'd cream down the creek bed on the snow-covered ice, checking traps, and it was like being in the middle of my own world where there wasn't anything else that mattered, just me and the traps.

And pretty? I don't know how to say it except that no artist, not even the good ones who get to do calendars and such, can come close to getting it down.

It's white, but blue somehow, and the cold—up to forty below, or should I say say down?—makes everything clean and new and crisp. When the moon is full and hits new snow it's like being in a ghost world where everything just *crackles* with cold, even your breath going out.

"Be so cold you can spit and watch it bounce," Harold said one night when I came in—it was the middle of the hard winter. "Must be fifty below."

I nodded. Even with my parka and sheepskin mittens and felt boots inside my shoepads I'd felt the cold. "I found a weasel that hadn't been trapped an hour, frozen stiff. You could pick him up by his tail."

"Be you checking the big line this weekend?" He looked at me across the table. "Even with the cold?"

"Yeah. I'll take plenty of matches."

"Should I worry if you don't come back at night?" He was watching me with a new look, one I didn't understand. Carl was already gone to Bonnie's, or I would have asked him about the look. It was like he was testing me or something.

I looked straight at him. "No, I don't think you have to worry if I spend the night. I know the woods, now." And it hit me that I wasn't lying, I really *did* know the woods.

It must have shown, because he threw me a short nod and held his cup out to Mildred. "Don't they grow fast?" he asked her. "Be he knows the woods, now, and it wasn't just a few months ago he couldn't find a tree if you stuck him under it."

She laughed and I went into the living room. We'd already eaten and it was time for the stories, which went on even without Carl, and I sat that night and listened to a story about a little French girl, only eight or nine, who ran a black market and made lots of money selling wine to the American soldiers when they came back from the trenches and had to drink.

Only it wasn't wine but vinegar mixed with wood alcohol and horse pee, and the soldiers went blind, some of them, and others went crazy, and when the story was over, Agile, who had told it, slapped his leg and laughed.

" 'Course I didn't drink any of it," he said, "being from the farm I could smell what it was. But them city boys drank it, and *didn't* they feel sorry later!"

I suppose it *was* a funny story, sort of, but halfway through it I started thinking about the Foxman, and the story wasn't funny anymore. It was sad. That a little girl would have to sell that to live, or that men went blind and crazy was sad. I laughed, only not really, just to be polite.

The next morning was Saturday and I took a can of soup and lots of matches, like I'd said I would, and the rifle and string to carry the pelts and rabbits I shot, and I started early, with the first good light.

The cold had made all the animals hole up, so

there wasn't much in the traps, and by early after-noon I'd come to the northernmost part of the line, where the loop started back to the farm.

I think I even turned around and aimed my skis back, but I'm not too sure. Whether I started back or not doesn't make any difference, because about ten minutes later I found myself going north like I'd been planning on doing it all the time—heading in the direction of the Foxman's shack.

It wasn't something I really meant to do, more like something I *had* to do, and I couldn't figure it at all except that it just felt right.

ELEVEN

On the way north I shot a couple of snowshoe rabbits, figuring I could at least bring some extra food. That was pretty silly, but I felt like I should bring something. Anything.

When I topped the rise I could see smoke coming out of the chimney, just like the time before, except that it was very still and the smoke went straight up, almost like a pointer.

I stopped for a minute, catching my wind from climbing the slope, then started down toward the shack. I'd gone about two hundred yards when he came out, probably to get wood, looked up and saw me, waved, and went back in the shack.

In a second he came out—he'd gone in for his mask—and went to the woodpile and started to split some birch.

I skied in and stopped. "Hi."

He sank the ax in the chopping block with a chunking sound and turned to me, his eyes bright above the black mask. "Where's the other one?"

"Oh, he's got a girl . . . well, that doesn't matter.

I came north on the line and thought if you didn't mind I'd come a little farther and see how you were doing."

"Did you, now."

"Well." I couldn't think of anything to say, "I brought a couple of rabbits." Really *dumb.*

He laughed, a whistling sound under the mask. "That's nice—very nice. Why don't you go ahead and clean 'em out and we'll have some stew. It's been some time since I had rabbit stew."

Yeah, I'll bet, I thought—probably two or three days. But he was nice to say that, and I could tell from his voice that he didn't mind my coming.

He went back to splitting birch and I used my belt knife to drop the guts out of the rabbits—back on the north side of the shack, where they'd freeze and he could use them for trap bait later. Then I jerked the skin—I mean I was really getting good at it, less than a minute to clean and skin a rabbit—and cut the heads off. I quartered them and wiped the meat with fresh snow to get all the hair and blood off, then carried them into the shack, where he was firing up the stove.

"They're fat rabbits," he said, by way of a compliment, when I put the meat on top of the stove in a pan. "Must have good feed south of here." He gestured with his head toward some split-wood cabinets to the right of the stove. "Shuck out of your coat and grab a cup—coffee's on the stove, sugar and spoon on the table."

I took off my parka and outside boots by the door and got a cup of coffee. I sat in the same chair as the time before, and looked at the same tablecloth, and wondered what I was doing there.

He must have been reading my mind, because I hadn't been sitting there three minutes when he chuckled over by the stove.

"Never thought I'd see you again," he said. "Not after the fright I gave you."

"It wasn't so bad—I mean . . ." I let it trail off.

"I know what you mean. It's all right. But if it isn't prying, just what are you doing here? This is a bit off the beaten path."

I thought about it for a minute. "I don't honestly know. I just wanted to see you, I guess, talk to you." I sat there, miserable, wishing I hadn't come.

"Some things like that," he cut in, "don't stand well to explaining. I know what you mean."

"It's like the skis." I laughed. "Just like the skis."

"What are you talking about?"

So I told him about Hans and how you couldn't look at the ski tips while they were drying or they wouldn't come out right and how there seemed to be a lot of things like that—things you couldn't see or dig at too much or it would ruin them.

"He's right—or you are. There are many things in life that die with explaining." He dumped the potatoes and meat into the stew pot and turned. "Science kills beauty, time and time again."

Which didn't make sense to me so I asked him to tell me what he meant, and he used the northern lights as an example.

"They have a ghostly beauty," he said. "A totally unreal quality that makes them beautiful in a mysterious way. Ancient man, and some Indians, worshiped them as a light from the gods."

I nodded—they would be easy to worship. When they came in on a bitter-cold night and splashed moving color all across the north sky, rolling from blue to red to green and back again, it was something to see. Took your breath away.

"But what if I told you that they were nothing but ionized particles in the upper stratosphere—purely a scientific phenomenon? That's what they are—just uncountable trillions of little particles being ionized. Nothing more."

"Yeah. I see what you mean." He was right, it did make them seem less pretty to think of them that way—not ugly, just less pretty. "I see what you mean."

"It's the same with everything. Science kills beauty—just like war destroys life."

His voice was rising a little, like he was getting mad or excited, standing over by the stove with his back to me, and it seemed a little strange that he would be getting mad, but I didn't say anything about it.

"How old are you?" he asked, suddenly.

"Fifteen—well, almost sixteen." I took a sip of coffee. "Why?"

"Because in a few years they'll be blowing the bugles again, just like they did when I was young—they *always* blow bugles. You'll be old enough to go when they do the next time. . . ." He let his voice trail off.

"So?"

"So nothing. Never mind." He turned away from the stove and picked up the guitar near the bed and sat down and started to play that Spanish music again, almost like I wasn't there. Sometimes people fight in themselves when they get mad, I've seen it before—do it myself—and I figured that's what he was doing. The flare-up in his voice was maybe a sign of it and he went to the guitar to work it out.

I sat quietly and listened to the music and it was clear that he was good—could really play. I didn't understand the music because it didn't go anywhere, like modern and rock and everything, but he never missed a note and just listening made me want to know more about the music.

The stew started to boil over, and since he didn't hear it I went over to the stove and moved it to a

cooler part of the top. I grabbed a spoon and stirred
it a couple of times to make sure it wouldn't stick.
The meat was starting to come apart and the smell
that came out of the pot reminded me that I hadn't
eaten since breakfast and my stomach rumbled
when I went back to the table.

He played for going on an hour, maybe a bit less,
then he stopped and put the guitar down.

"You'll spend the night," he said, and it wasn't
a question but an order put in a nice way.

I nodded. "If it's all right."

"Tomorrow I'll take you out and show you how
to trap fox—before you go."

"Sure. Thanks."

Then he picked up the guitar again, because the
stew wasn't done and wouldn't be done for maybe
another hour, and he played and played and I listened while I thought of him sitting alone here all
winter and summer, year after year since before I
was born and then some, and I wondered if he
played the guitar when nobody was around to hear
but the woods.

Once he looked up and his eyes smiled over the
mask and he said, "Thank you. For coming."

I was going to say something but it got caught,
because his eyes looked so nice and the music was
making me sappy, all mushy inside; I was going
to tell him that I came for me, more than for him,
because he had something I wanted, only I didn't

know what it was. But it didn't come out, so I just nodded. "I'm glad I came," I said, and meant it.

"Tomorrow," he repeated, "we'll trap some fox."

And I guess it was another way of saying thank you because his eyes were all misted over, as if he might start to cry; and the next thing I knew I was bawling all by myself, sitting at the table thinking about how lonely he must get, *alone* lonely, if a kid coming to visit him would make him that happy.

But I hid it and he didn't see me cry, which is just as well because the crying was pretty dumb even if the reason wasn't.

TWELVE

We were out at first light. I'd slept on the floor, though he'd insisted I take his bed again. Thing is, whatever else he was, the Foxman was old and he needed a bed more than I needed one, so he finally listened to reason.

We'd had coffee and strip steaks from the moose carcass hanging on the north side of the shack, where it would keep all winter, and I had a warm lump in my belly the size of my fist when we went out.

Lucky I did, too, because it was colder than I'd ever seen it up there; like something solid coming down from the north.

You could hear trees exploding off in the woods. The sap in them froze until the wood couldn't hold it anymore and then *crack*, like a cannon going off, the trees exploded.

I got onto my skis and the Foxman pulled down a set of long snowshoes that he'd made out of birch and rawhide.

"Skis are all right," he said, standing on the

shoes and shuffling to make sure they were on tight enough. "I just never got used to them."

The steam from his breath lifted the mask when he talked and made it look like he was smoking. He turned and started north and I followed, my skis riding easily on the snow packed by his shoes.

He had about fifteen or twenty traps hanging from a pole, so they'd stay away from his body and not pick up the man-smell, and they clanked as he walked, a sharp sound in the morning.

We went a mile without stopping or talking, the traps clanking away, when we came onto a small stream all frozen over and covered with snow.

"Here," he said, and stopped. "They always hunt streambeds in the winter and meadows in the summer."

"Why is that?"

"Because fox are smart, and in the winter a streambed is easier to hunt because the snow freezes and packs on the ice and makes traveling easier; in the summer the meadows are the easiest."

"If they're so smart, how can we trap them?"

He snorted a laugh. "Good point—we use their own devious minds to catch them."

I waited, but he didn't say anything more and I followed him down into the streambed and across to where the bank came down with a small overhang.

Back in, under the overhang, he put a trap with some frozen rabbit guts for bait—all set and out in the open.

"You're kidding," I said. "There's no *way* a fox is going to get in that trap."

Another laugh cut the morning. "You're absolutely right—but watch."

On top of the overhang he dug down in the snow and put another trap in and covered it lightly with snow—using sticks for all the work so he wouldn't leave a smell. Then he moved away, went back in the brush ten or fifteen feet where an opening led away from the stream, and put another trap down, covered with snow.

"What's that for?"

"This, my boy, is the trap that gets us the fox."

"Then what about all this other stuff?" I waved a hand at the set with the bait and the trap on the overhang.

"All for show." He pointed upstream. "Old daddy fox comes down the river and smells the bait, which he knows is a setup, then he finds the trap on the overhang. So he decides to go out and around, come in from another way, and that's when we nail him."

"Does it really work like that?"

He nodded. "Every time. You just use the cunning of the fox against him."

We went upstream about a mile and he laid five

more sets, until all his traps were gone, and by that time it was coming on midday and time to get back for a bit of lunch before I headed back for the farm.

We ate in silence, except for the sounds he made, which I was getting used to and didn't bother me anymore. When we finished I did the dishes while he "hotted up" some coffee, which is how he put it, then we sat for a cup before I left.

"Those people at the farm, they're not your folks, are they?"

I shook my head. "Uncle and aunt—on my mother's side."

"They treat you all right?"

I nodded. "Yeah—they're great. Except, well, nothing really."

"Except what?"

"Oh, it's no big thing." I was going to tell him about the stories, the war stories Hans and Agile told every night, but I caught myself in time. It hit me that he probably didn't want to hear anything about the war—anything nice, at any rate. "It's nothing. Something I've got to work out myself."

His eyes smiled over the mask. "There are things like that—to work out for yourself."

I stood up. "I guess I should be going, if I'm going to get back before it's too late."

He nodded. "Yes. They'll be worried if you don't show."

"Well."

I turned and started for the door, where my coat and boots were, and worked into them.

"It was good of you to come." His voice was tight and I turned. "I mean, it was good to see you. Again."

"About that—I was wondering if you'd mind me coming back next weekend." It slipped out before I knew it was coming, but I meant it, so I let it ride, even though I still didn't know why I wanted to come.

"Be good to have you," he said. "And that other boy, Carl, if he wants to come. Him, too."

"He's pretty well locked into this girl he's seeing, but I'll ask."

"Whatever—I'll see you next week."

I nodded and went out, got into my skis and started south in the slant afternoon sun. At the top of the rise I looked back and he waved from the shack, and I waved before I dropped down out of sight.

It didn't take as long to get home as usual, because I was getting to know all the shortcuts and easy paths, plus I skipped checking some traps, so I made it for dinner in plenty of time, and I had a couple of weasels that I took out of traps on the way home to show for my effort.

After supper we went into the living room—everybody but Carl, who was gone, of course—and Agile told a story about a time when they were at the front and they couldn't get any food, so they ate some meat they bought from a buy that wasn't so bad and it was supposed to be horsemeat.

Only it wasn't from horses, it was from rats, which was sort of like the story about the wine. Everybody laughed except Mildred, who shivered a little and looked like she might be going to get sick.

And of course me. I didn't laugh either. I didn't even smile, though I knew it was impolite, because I was thinking of the Foxman almost all the way through the story and I didn't think it was funny that men had to eat rats to keep from starving.

But they didn't notice, not even Agile, who had told the story and would watch the audience because it was his story.

They didn't see me not laugh.

THIRTEEN

"I can't handle it—I can't sit and listen to the stories anymore." I was sitting in the shack the next weekend sipping coffee. "I wasn't going to talk about it, but I thought maybe if we sat and talked for a while . . ."

The Foxman was sitting back on his bed with his guitar. We'd just eaten dinner—two grouse that I'd nailed on the way over, baked with potatoes and some peas from a can—and he'd started to play while I sat at the table.

"You're talking around it," he said.

"What do you mean?"

He struck a chord on the guitar and put it back in the corner in its case. "I mean what you really want to know is what happened to my face."

I shook my head, hard. "No. I don't want to pry or anything. It's just that I sit at the farm and listen to the stories from Agile and Hans about the war and how great it all was . . ."

"Have you ever heard of Verdun?" he asked, holding up a hand to stop me. "In France?"

"No—well, yes, but not really. I know it was a place where they fought a big battle during World War One."

"It was more than that." He laughed bitterly. "Much more. It was the ultimate of science killing beauty; the triumph of machines over flesh." He waved a hand at the books. "It made everything in those books, all human knowledge, worthless in a way."

"How do you mean?" I was getting to know his voice, now, and the look in his eyes above the mask, and I could tell when he was getting mad or excited. Like now. "How did it make all knowledge worthless?"

"Iron, my boy—steel against flesh, science against beauty. The beauty of being human. And beauty lost. At Verdun they rained iron from the skies, rained death for months on end, killed men by the thousands and maimed them by the thousands until nothing was left but bones. And steel. It was to be the battle to end all battles. . . ." He let it slide off into nothing.

"But there was another war—the Second World War." I was looking at the tablecloth and the flowers and I didn't know why. "Another war, and now Korea."

But he wasn't listening. His eyes were closed, and there was moistness at the corners. "Steel—so much steel in the ground that even now, all these years later, nothing will grow in Verdun. Not even grass will grow in Verdun. Only steel, and bones."

His voice was so quiet I could barely hear it, and when he stopped talking he just stopped—like something inside him quit moving. I looked up and he still had his eyes closed, remembering, and I wanted to be able to help him but I didn't know how.

"Tell me about the *world,* boy!"

He said it sudden and loud, so it rang in the shack, and I jumped. "What do you mean?"

Then his eyes opened and he looked at me and the smile was back. "Sorry. I was thinking of a time and place that you couldn't understand and should never have to understand."

I didn't say anything because it was obvious he didn't want an answer or any more questions.

"These stories that you're hearing back at the farm—don't let them get you down. All they're trying to do is pluck a rose from manure."

"Pardon?"

"The men telling those stories are only trying to remember some of the parts of the war that might be worth remembering—trying to find some use in all that waste."

I thought about it, nodded. "Maybe. But I can't understand how they can even *think* about it being funny when you . . . well."

"I know, I know." He let his voice go soft and low. "But they have to try, they have to try or it was all for nothing, and nobody likes to do something all for nothing."

And that's the last we talked about the stories Hans and Agile told, that night and forever, and from then on I tried to understand the stories and worked very hard at looking underneath the surface of what they were saying; I looked for the rose they were trying to pluck from the manure.

I'd like to say I found it, that I could see and feel what they really meant with the stories, but I didn't, couldn't. I never saw the rose.

The truth is that I kind of drifted away from the farm and the people at the farm, all of them, and started being more with myself—and I spent more time with the Foxman.

Carl was gone all the time anyway and didn't notice—he was talking of living happily ever after with Bonnie, which I can understand for someone older but not Carl. But then I've never been that hooked in love, so there's no way to tell what it was doing to him. It just sounded dumb to me.

But if Carl didn't notice anything, Harold did, and when I'd been going out to the Foxman's for over two months—at the end of February—he took me aside in the barn one night after chores.

"Be you not happy here?" He offered me snoose

so I'd know he wasn't mad but being nice. "Living with us?"

It shocked me because I thought I'd kept it hidden. "No. I love it here—maybe even better than home."

"But you go all the time—every weekend, into the brush. Be like you're trying to get away from us or something."

"It's just the woods," I said. "I like being in the woods. I've got a little lean-to out there and I don't mind being alone. The woods are nice." I said it all a little fast, but it was mostly true—I *did* like the woods—and he accepted it.

"So, good," he said, nodding. "Be something does bother you, you'll tell me." His eyebrows were raised, making it a question, and I nodded and told him that if something did bother me he'd be the first to know. He didn't bring it up again.

That night Hans told a story about a man he knew in the war who'd been shot up pretty bad so it was obvious he would die, wouldn't make it through the night, and he wanted some good champagne, only there wasn't any in the area.

So Hans and another soldier got some water and sugar and worked half the night making champagne—with a lot of other ingredients—and when they finally got it done and took it in to the dying man, it was too late. He was already dead.

So they sold the champagne they'd made to some Moroccan soldiers in the next set of trenches.

"And don't you know they got drunk on it?" Hans said, finishing the story. "Drunk as skunks, all of them, and there wasn't a *drop* of alcohol in the stuff. It was all in their heads."

And I couldn't find the rose that time, either, only the manure. All I could think of was the soldier who died before he could taste the wine.

FOURTEEN

Sometimes it would be nice if life just kept happening the way it's happening, if things got to a good place and just stayed there, didn't change.

Like the next two months—they were perfect for me. Well, maybe perfect is too strong a word, but they were the best I'd had in a long time and maybe the best I'll ever have. School was easy, because it was small and the teacher had to spread around so much that she didn't have time to make it hard, and because the Foxman was helping me on everything but math. Which he thought wasn't worth learning unless you were going into a way of life that takes knowledge of numbers.

I went there every weekend, and once we got used to each other, got over trying to understand each other, I guess, it was great. I didn't talk about the stories anymore, because it didn't seem to do any good, and he got away from the war thing and got me into his books and taught me how to see some things I couldn't see.

Actually he just taught me new ways to look at

the same old things, taught me always to question things and make sure they were right before accepting them. Like in history, how things aren't always what they seem to be.

"Always ask the second question," he told me one night after we'd eaten moose roast and I could still taste the tallow on my lips like chap salve or something. "Don't just ask why, but *why* why?"

"What do you mean?" It was a question I found myself asking more and more when I visited the Foxman. In front of me on the table I had a book covering the American Revolution and I pointed to the pages. "Isn't this the truth?"

He nodded. "Of course. But it wasn't necessarily complete. By reading that, you'll learn the why of American Revolution, but it doesn't answer the second question—why the why of the American Revolution?"

Which was vague, of course, and made me wonder what he was talking about, but that was the way he did things. Leave you wondering a little, like being thirsty when you'd just finished drinking, so you'd want to drink more. I'm still not sure about the second-question business, just what he meant, but I turned in a paper at school on the American Revolution that the teacher said was the best she'd ever seen, and that's not so bad even if it was a small school.

When we weren't going through his books or he

wasn't playing music, we worked his line for fox. And he took them right and left, smart as they were—the Foxman knew the woods better than anybody I'd ever seen, better even than Harold or Hans or Agile.

I guess it was because he'd lived there so long that he was part of it all, the way I'd heard of some woodsies getting when they stay back in the brush for a long time. Once when I was skiing back to the farm on a Sunday afternoon and my mind wasn't on hunting or anything, I figured out that the Foxman had been in the woods for over thirty years, most of it in the same cabin, and in that long a time you can learn a lot about where you live.

Like I could read sign pretty well—you show me a set of tracks and I could walk them down and give you the animal if I had the time.

But you put the Foxman on a set and he could tell you the animal, how old it was, the last time it had eaten, whether or not it was sick, if it was running scared or in a hurry and when it would bed down. From one set of tracks.

And he could smell things. Really. Where I had to use my eyes and ears, he could *smell* an animal, sometimes almost feel it.

One Saturday afternoon, late, we were skiing and snowshoeing through a small stand of poplars. It was a warm day, up to thirty above, and I'd just opened my parka to cool down a little when the

Foxman drew up and held his hand to stop me.

"They're here." He felt tense and stiff standing there.

"What?"

"They're here—all around us, in the snow."

For just a minute I thought he'd gone crazy. He had that same tight feeling he had sometimes when he got excited. But no, this time it was the woods thing, the animal thing.

I started looking around, blurring my vision so objects would stand out the way he'd taught me, and back in the underbrush, the low red willows, I saw grouse all around us. Of course as soon as I saw them they exploded up and out in that thunder they make that scares you even when you're ready for it.

"How did you know they were there?" I asked, when they'd all flown out of sight.

"Smelled them."

And he had, too. Another time we were making our way across a clearing when he turned and grabbed me by the sleeve and pulled me, on my skis, as fast as we could go the rest of the way across the clearing.

"What . . . ?" I almost fell over trying to keep up with him.

"Quiet! Quiet now and you'll see something!"

So we crouched in back of a spruce and waited

and in a couple of minutes a moose came out, a bull but with his antlers gone, and he was fine to see. He had the red eye and was mad at nothing and everything, the way moose get, and he plowed into that clearing in deep snow and he didn't look real, more like something from a dream, maybe a nightmare or a wild movie. He snorted and bellowed so the whole woods knew he was a moose, and if you didn't like it you could just come out into that clearing and he'd talk it over with you.

I couldn't say anything, not even after he was gone and all that was left was the gouge in the snow where he'd come into the clearing. I was thinking of a painting I'd seen once, of a bunch of dinosaurs—that's what the moose made me think about. Something prehistoric—something you're not supposed to see.

"How was that, my boy?" He whispered it when the moose was gone, the way you whisper in a library. Or a church. "How was that?"

"Beautiful—no, more than that. Unbelievable." I looked up at him, the eyes glistening over the mask. "How did you know he was coming?"

"Felt him—just knew it. I can't explain it except that it's like knowing what somebody is going to say just before they say it. I just knew he was coming and we had to get out of that clearing."

Those two months were full of things like that,

beautiful and strange learning things that I can't really explain because you almost had to be part of it to understand what it was like.

I didn't want it to end, like I said, and it could have just stayed that way—even with the stories from Agile and Hans—for the rest of my life and I wouldn't have cared.

But life has a way of pulling the rug out from under you just when you need it least, which is what they like to call growing, I guess, but as far as I'm concerned you can have it.

It seems like everything they call growing up has to jerk your guts out and just about wreck you and I've never been able to understand why that's supposed to be good for you.

It's dumber than falling in love and freezing your ears until the lobes almost fall off.

FIFTEEN

It's strange, how things happen and they don't turn out like you think they will. Going on the end of March I went blind, snow-blind, and it was pretty bad. But I didn't think it would kill the Foxman.

Which is what it did, and even when I look back on it now and try to see something I could have changed, or a way I could have known it was going to happen, I don't see it. There was no way to tell it was going to happen the way it happened, no way to stop it, really, even if I'd known it was coming.

It was early spring, the last part of March, and while the snow was still pretty deep it was melting and freezing so it was like ice—all glistening and shiny when the sun hit it. You could almost walk on it without skis, it was so hard, and it made the trip over to the Foxman's twice as fast. That, coupled with the fact that there wasn't much trapping because the animals were mostly out of prime and losing their good coats meant that I could spend more time with him on the weekends, and maybe that was the reason that I was beginning to love him.

Not in a mushy way, of course, but more like he was taking over where my folks left off when they started drinking years before. I asked him things, and he always gave me an answer I could live with and which usually turned out to be right, or at least got me on the right track, and that's a kind of love. Having somebody do that for you.

Which made what happened a lot harder to live with, I can tell you.

I started early in the morning in the last weekend in March and that was a mistake. The sun was in my eyes, coming up off that melted snow-ice like off a mirror, almost hot, and I had to squint even to see my ski tips. But bright sun on snow wasn't new to me, so I didn't think much of it, just screwed my eyes a little tighter and kept going.

What I didn't know is that conditions were perfect for going snow-blind, and that I was making it worse by heading into the rising morning sun.

I also didn't know that the worst storm of the year was coming; a big-daddy killer storm from the north that would leave over thirty people dead in Minnesota alone, frozen to death, some of them hanging on fences and others just sitting in their cars.

I just kept skiing toward the Foxman's shack,

jumping a rabbit now and then, and once a fox that I could have dropped easy but let go because he was losing his winter coat and wouldn't have been worth skinning.

About noon I stopped for a breather. It was only two or three more miles to the Foxman's but I didn't want to waste my energy. In the woods you always keep a little back—that's what the Foxman had taught me—because if you go till you're really tired you might find that you need some extra strength just when you don't have it.

Twice I'd had to rub my eyes because they were running tears, but I could still see all right and figured it was the wind—there was a little breeze out of the south—and other than that there was no indication of what was coming. Just the tears and a little burning.

But when I'd finished my break and started to get back into my skis I noticed that I had to squint to see the bindings, and that it seemed a little darker, like maybe a cloud had covered the sun, only when I looked up there wasn't any cloud.

I shrugged it off, which was just about the worst thing I could do, because in the woods a small thing can snowball until it kills you—you should always believe the sign, always believe and pay attention to what's happening around or to you, or it will get out of hand and come down on you like a ton of bricks.

I hadn't gone twenty yards, probably less, when it hit me that I couldn't see my ski tips. They were lost in a kind of reddish blur. I stopped and rubbed my eyes and it didn't do any good.

Then I looked down and I couldn't see my feet, and I held my hands out and couldn't see them even though I knew they were just inches from my face. I was blind. Stone-blind, as blind as a post.

And right when it hit me that I was blind it felt some somebody had dumped a five-gallon bucket of sand in my eyes—all cutting grit, and I went a little crazy.

They say a lot of things in books about panicking in the woods, and how you shouldn't do it, but most of the people who write those things are sitting in a quiet living room while they write, with the heater humming and maybe some hot coffee next to them. When you're warm and comfortable and happy, it's easy to say don't panic in the woods.

When you're alone in the brush and suddenly find yourself stone-blind, panic is the first thing that comes to mind. It's just like all those books had never been written.

I crashed through the brush like a crazy man. Or maybe I should say I tried to, because I ran into trees and got knocked down and I'd get up and try again and get knocked down again. I think I screamed some, before I started using my brain, and I know I bashed my face on a tree of some kind because I could feel the blood running from my nose down around my mouth.

I lost my rifle right away—the only way I had of signaling any distance—and I finally wound up sitting at the base of a tree with my head down on my arms, crying.

Just like that. I figured I was blind for good, not knowing much about going snow-blind, and that it usually lasted only a day or two, and there wasn't any way I could handle it.

And then the sounds came. Things I'd never heard before, or hadn't noticed because I could see; little cracks and creaks from the brush, all sounding like something coming toward me. Maybe wolves and even knowing that wolves aren't bad, don't bother people, my mind started working on how they could come in and tear me to pieces because I couldn't see to stop them. Or a moose could come down on me and I wouldn't know it until he had me. Dumb thinking like that, and the panic started up again and I had to fight it down, had to think.

So I was blind—that's what I thought—but what did I have going for me? I'd lost my rifle and one ski, which didn't help, but I could still think.

The wind was from the south, and I turned my

face to feel it. It was still there, and if I made my way with the wind at my back, took it slow, I'd be heading north, in the direction of the shack.

So I started out like that, stumbling and feeling my way, trying to keep the wind at my back, and it was slow and hard but I made some ground— maybe a hundred yards every half hour although I had no way of knowing time or distance. It was like being inside a red room that didn't have any corners and ended just inside your eyes.

I'd been working that way for a couple of hours, and thought I might be getting close enough to the shack to start yelling so maybe the Foxman would hear me, when I noticed that the wind coming from my back was getting colder. Much colder. And there were little spits of water hitting my face, snowflakes, which was strange because snowflakes hardly ever come with a south wind.

Snow comes with a north wind.

I stopped, and what had happened hit me like a hammer between the eyes. The wind had worked around to the north, and I'd been using the wind for a guide, keeping it at my back. I'd made a circle.

And there was a storm coming. How bad it would be I couldn't tell, but the wind was picking up all the time and the snow was getting thicker on my face and I think I would have panicked again, run nuts again, except that I was too tired from stumbling through the snow. Too tired by a mile.

I was whipped, done and done. There was no way of knowing where I was, how far I'd circled, from which direction the wind was really coming. No way to know how to get anywhere but where I was—alone, blind, in a storm in the middle of the woods.

Too tired really to care one way or the other, I moved until I felt the branches of a spruce catch my face and I crawled under them and pulled my parka as tight as I could around me, until the wind quit coming in, and hunkered down.

Sleep came first, I knew that from talking to people who'd found bodies. I knew I couldn't go to sleep, and I fought it for a long time while the wind kept getting stronger and the snow came thicker and thicker. I fought sleep as hard as I could.

But I was shot tired, and it all seemed like a waste of effort, somehow; like why should I fight sleep so hard when it would make me forget I was blind and was probably going to freeze to death anyway?

So I let it come, after a long time, and it wasn't so bad. Not nearly as bad as they say it is   just kind of gray and warm and loose. Like a quilt it came, and I let it, and the last thing I remember was the wind making a tearing sound in the branches of the spruce.

SIXTEEN

Somebody was pulling at me, jerking me around, and I got mad and tried to shove him away. It was nice where I was, asleep under the tree, and I didn't want to be disturbed. I pushed at the hands that kept trying to shake me awake, pull me out from under the tree.

"Come on, boy. You can't stay here, you'll die." The voice came from miles away, sounded hollow, and I recognized it as the Foxman's but it didn't seem real, more like a dream. "Come on, boy, get up!"

I opened my eyes, but I was still blind and only saw the red blush. "Go away. Leave me alone." I thought I said it aloud, but the wind was roaring now, thundering through the trees, and the sound was carried away. "Leave me alone."

He pushed and tugged until I was on my hands and knees and I fought him all the way, fought to get back into that gray world where the pain in my hands and feet didn't matter, would go away.

"No, boy. You've got to live." He kept pulling until I finally got to my feet, out from under the tree, and he made me stomp and clap until I could feel blood moving again in my legs and arms; blood that felt like fire and hurt so bad I wanted to scream.

"I'm blind!" I screamed at him, to get over the wind sound. "I can't see!" I could feel the snow hitting the parts of my face that could still feel—weren't numb with cold—and it was being driven like needles.

"Hang on to my coat," he said, leaning and yelling into my ear. "Just hang on to my coat."

He started out and I staggered after him, stiff-legged and stumbling like a drunk. We went that way for what seemed like hours and he stopped.

"Got to take a break!" he yelled. "Just for a minute." Then he coughed and even over the wind I could hear that the cough came from someplace deep in his chest. The cold was getting to him.

"What time is it?" I asked, but I had to repeat it twice before he heard.

"Coming up on the middle of the night. I've been looking for you since this afternoon."

Then he started walking again and I followed him, and what seemed like hours more but was probably only forty minutes I felt the wind stop suddenly as we came up to the side of the shack.

He led me inside and dropped me on the bed, then tore my clothes off and rubbed my legs and arms.

"I'm blind," I said, over and over. "I can't see." I knew I was babbling but I couldn't stop it and I just kept saying it.

"I know, I know." His voice was soothing and low, the way people who know animals talk to them to quiet them down, and after a time I quit chattering away and he finished rubbing me and covered me with the bearskin. Then I heard him clanking around on the stove, coughing that same deep cough, and in a little while he came back to the bed and put something on my eyes.

"Leave them," he said, pulling my hands back down when I tried to reach up. "They're used tea bags. You'll be able to see in a couple of hours."

"What happened to my eyes?"

"Snow-blind. The ice crystals in the snow caught the sun just right and you didn't know it was coming."

"I was afraid."

"I know, I know." He made his voice soothing again. "Don't worry—it's all over now. A little sleep and you'll be as good as new."

"I was alone."

He rubbed my forehead. "I know, I know. It's all right now."

"How did you find me?"

"Luck—and the fact that God smiled on you." He chuckled. "I had given up, figured maybe you decided not to come, and started back and I was swearing some at you. I thought you'd gotten a girl and quit coming, but I had to look—what with the storm and all."

I thought about him working the woods in that storm. Even in the shack the wind was almost deafening.

"So I started back, and I hadn't gone half a mile when I tripped on something in the snow."

"My rifle."

"No. Your ski—the tip got caught in the front of my right snowshoe. Of course then I knew you were around and just started working circles until I found you underneath the tree."

Something boiled on the stove and he brought me a cup that was so hot I couldn't hold it.

"Moose-fat broth," he said, holding the cup to my lips. "Drink it hot so it gets down."

I swallowed it and felt it burn all the way down. It was rich and thick.

"And now," he said, taking the cup away, "you go to sleep." He coughed again and seemed to have trouble stopping and I asked him about the cough.

"It's nothing to worry about. You go to sleep."

I leaned back on the pillow, settled in. I heard him thunking around back in the corner and pretty soon the guitar music came. It was an old French lullaby he'd played for me before, and it did the trick because in ten seconds I went under like a drowning man going down for the third time.

The dream came right away, the dream about the storm and almost freezing to death, and it was very real—almost as real as what had happened. When I got to the part where I was panicking I awakened a little and looked over to the table. The Foxman was coughing again and I wanted to help him, but I couldn't stay awake and slipped back under.

When I finally did awaken it was daylight, and that's when I realized I could see again—I'd missed it during the night when I saw the Foxman at the table and aside from a little burning in the corners, my eyes seemed fine.

The Foxman was out of the room, outside, and I swung my feet to the floor just as he came in with an armload of wood.

"You're awake," he said, putting the wood in the woodbox. "How do you feel?"

"Fine," I answered. And I did feel fine, too. "It's like nothing ever happened."

He nodded. "That's how it hits—quick and gone. Another two or three hours and you'd have been dead—I found you just in time."

"About that—I was dumb out there, in the woods. Really dumb. Thank you for saving me."

He laughed and it made the mask billow out and back. "It just happened—don't pick at it."

"Well. Just so you know I learned a lesson."

He started to say something but the coughing hit him and he had to hunch over. It sounded really rough.

"That doesn't sound good," I said. "It comes from deep."

"Ahh, it's nothing. I've had it before and it goes away."

"Still—take something for it."

He nodded. "Yes—I will. Don't worry about me."

But I did worry. It worked at me while we ate, and then later when I left to go back to the farm, where they were ready to call out a search party for me—all the way through the new snow with the snow goggles the Foxman had given me, I worried about that cough.

I shouldn't have left him alone, and I can see that now. But then I was caught between the rock and the hard place. If I stayed, Carl would bring Harold out and I knew the Foxman didn't want anybody else to know he was there. Not anybody. He'd said it hundreds of times.

"They'll come and the next thing they'll feel sorry for me," he'd said. "I don't want that."

So I had to leave, had to go back to the farm even though I knew it was wrong. I had to leave him in the shack alone even though it was the last thing in the world I wanted to do, because that's what he wanted.

But I worried about that cough.

SEVENTEEN

It was spring break that week, and because of the storm I didn't have to make school Monday. Nobody at the farm noticed that my rifle was gone, so aside from asking me how the storm had gone for me in the lean-to, Harold didn't know or care about what had happened to me. I didn't tell him I'd gone snow-blind, of course, and I hid the goggles so he wouldn't find them and ask questions.

Monday morning after chores I asked if it was all right if I went into the woods. Harold gave me a funny look but said it was fine, so I left.

I made the best time, new snow and all, that I'd ever made getting over to the Foxman's shack and didn't even stop for a break, to save a little strength, but still I was too late.

When I came over the rise I could see there wasn't any smoke coming out of the chimney on the shack. Which could have meant that he was out on his line, and I prayed for that as I busted through the snow, but I knew he wasn't out because there wasn't anything to trap until the ice

113

went out on the streams and he could take beaver, and it wasn't the time of the year to be hunting for meat. Not in spring, when everything was new. You hunted for meat in the fall, when the new time was over—that's how he'd told it to me.

All of this was running through my head as I went for the shack, and when I got there and jerked out of my bindings and opened the door I kind of knew what I was going to find before I found it. I could feel it, smell it, the way the Foxman felt the moose.

He was back in the corner on the bed, under the bearskin, with the guitar laid across him and I thought he was dead then, because the shack was as cold as a tomb inside and it must have been all night since he had a fire going.

But when I came in and thumped the door closed he moved, just a little, so I knew he was still alive. I went to the stove and fired it up, jacked in a bunch of narrow-split birch so it would burn hot, and then went over to the bed.

It wasn't pretty, but then I thought of him coming out into the storm to get me and how he looked didn't matter so much. He had his mask off, and next to his head was a towel and he'd been coughing blood into the towel.

"Hello, boy," he said, or tried to say, but it brought the coughing again and I could see the pain from his chest come up into his eyes.

I went back to the stove and put some water to boil, threw some tea bags into it and returned to the bed.

"There'll be tea in a minute," I said. "You rest for now."

He nodded and lay back, and I pulled a chair from the table over to the edge of the bed and sat down next to his head.

I didn't know what to do, how to help. It came to me that I should maybe go for outside help, because he didn't look like he was going to make it without a doctor, but then if I left he might not last until I could get back. So I just sat, and hoped and prayed for him, which is maybe pretty dumb, but I prayed to whatever it was that had let him find me in the storm, whatever that luck had been, because it was pretty powerful, and in a little while he opened his eyes.

"You're still here."

I nodded. He got it out without coughing and I thought maybe my prayers were working. That was silly, but I was grabbing at anything.

"Yes, I'm still here. I'll stay as long as it takes, as long as you need me. . . ."

"I went back," he cut in. "I went back to France in my mind, back before I was gassed. I was young then, and beautiful in a way."

I didn't say anything.

"There was a girl then, named Claudine, and we

115

would go out in the flowers." He closed his eyes. "There was beauty then—beauty and love. Then it all went to hell."

He reached out with a hand and I took it. It felt like old leather, and was cold, and the cold frightened me because it was like the hand was already dead. But I held it, and he squeezed hard, so hard I thought my fingers would break.

"The books are for you, and the hides. All of it. For you." He started coughing again. "Burn the shack, with me in it."

"Don't die." I know how dumb that sounds, but that's what I said, and then I said it over and over like it was a song. "Don't die, don't die, don't die."

But it didn't work. He kept squeezing my hand and finally he said, "I know . . . I *know* what it is now, what it's supposed to be. . . ." But he never finished whatever it was he knew because he just quit talking and his eyes stayed open, open and wide, and the pressure on my hand stopped.

And he died.

I sat for a while and cried, holding his hand, and I wished I could have been and done more, the way you do, and then I moved away from him, because he was gone, and I put the guitar next to him and emptied the kerosine lamp around the floor of the cabin and dropped a match in the puddle.

It caught slow because the floor was cold, but

then it got going and I grabbed my coat and boots and went outside. I wasn't going to take anything, because it was all *him* somehow, and shouldn't be seen by other people because he wanted to be alone even if that wasn't true.

Which I can see now. But then I was a little crazy and thought there should be no trace of him left for them to pity; nothing for them to see or know about after what they'd done to him.

But then I decided I should have something for myself and I took a foxhide off the wall before the flames came through. Then I moved away from the shack and watched it burn, to make sure it wouldn't spread into the woods, and when it had burned all the way down I threw some birch from the woodpile onto it to make sure it would burn long enough to get the job done, so there wouldn't be any trace of him for them to find and pity. I didn't know who they were right then, but I hated them anyway and didn't want to leave anything of him for them.

And when it was done I took the foxhide and got on my skis and skied back to the farm, without looking back once because what was there to see but ashes?

And that night when Carl and I were up in bed I told him about it, about the storm and the Foxman and how he was dead now, and Carl said man, that's rough, and I agreed. And then Carl told me

117

that he and Bonnie had decided that even though they were in love and could wait it would be all right to go all the way and she was two months pregnant.

Yeah. Like it didn't matter that the Foxman was dead. I got madder than hell and told Carl I didn't care if she had a *goat*, which got him hot and we fought, only not really—quiet-like so Mildred wouldn't hear us.

Afterward I rolled over to go to sleep, which was impossible, and I was lying there thinking about the Foxman and half crying in the dark when Carl took my shoulder.

"Hey. I mean it was rough about the old man. I mean that."

"Yeah. I know."

"I'm sorry we fought."

"It's all right—it didn't mean anything."

And that was the end of it except that the next week Harold told me there'd been a fire back in the woods, an old shack burned down, and he asked if I knew anything about it.

I said I didn't and he dropped it, even though he gave me that look again, the one that meant he knew something and wouldn't talk about it.

That same night Agile told a story about the war, and it was a funny one and everybody laughed and I tried really hard to find the rose that Agile was plucking from the manure, the thing he was trying to save in all the waste, but I couldn't. I could only see the waste, only the manure.

Which was probably my own fault because I wasn't really listening to the story anyway. I was thinking of the Foxman all the while Agile talked, and I still do that when we listen to the stories and it helps. Not a lot, but it helps some, and if that doesn't work I go up to the room and run my fingers through the hair on the fox pelt I took from the shack.

It's beautiful fur, red and rich and deep, almost as beautiful as the Foxman.